About the Author

Dave Gregson worked for nearly 25 years in the health, social care and charity sectors. After being dismissed following bullying, intimidation and poor practice, Dave won his legal case for unfair dismissal. The case was relatively high profile and received much press coverage. Dave has since set himself up as an inclusion and equalities campaigner and volunteer for several causes such as workplace bullying, autism awareness, safeguarding and animal welfare. Dave has also volunteered in promoting tolerance and cultural understanding and has spent time in North Korea, Afghanistan and Iraq, amongst other countries. Since winning the case, Dave has also turned to writing and is a registered unpaid carer for family; he is very vocal in supporting unpaid carers' rights.

Nothing of Interest

Dave Gregson

Nothing of Interest

Olympia Publishers
London

www.olympiapublishers.com
OLYMPIA PAPERBACK EDITION

A CIP catalogue record for this title is
available from the British Library.

ISBN: 978-1-80074-179-9

This is a work of fiction.
Names, characters, places and incidents originate from the writer's
imagination. Any resemblance to actual persons, living or dead, is
purely coincidental.

First Published in 2021

Olympia Publishers
Tallis House
2 Tallis Street
London
EC4Y 0AB

Printed in Great Britain

Dedication

To my father, Terence Gregson, the best storyteller of all time who taught me everything that I had to learn about the art of creating stories.

Acknowledgements

Thanks to all the team at Olympia Publishers, the members of the Society of Authors, the illustrator, Samuel Batley, and the proofreader, Craig Smith of CRS Editorial and Aimee Youles. My parents, John, Beth and Esme, Catherine, Stu; all my friends and family and my cat.

Nothing of Interest

An astronaut learned early to treat the natural world with respect. Differences, strangeness, even the bizarre, are the norm. Exploration with minimal intrusion and dislocation—the notion that 'we' are the 'guests'. That is the basic galactic protocol. But it is not always seen that way from the other side. A perceived threat, real or not, and animate nature fights back and with an impressive variety of weaponry. Captain MacGregor, of Odyssey II, an experienced pilot, still had quite a bit to learn. Plus a lot to learn to forget.

It was a routine mission. An exploratory probe in a remote sector of the 'Silent Quarter' to carry out a scientific survey of a tiny planetoid known as X16. Part of a rather grand project to investigate and document all the more distant stretches of the accessible universe—to record, catalogue and, where possible, recover specimens of flora and fauna. As Captain, MacGregor occasionally reflected on the irresistible human compulsion to quantify and classify each distinction. Every dot, comma and crossed 't'. Still, mustn't grumble, it had given him a lucrative career.

It was practically the end of an exhausting tour of duty. Seven months away from earth, family, friends, civilised company, drink—and all the etc. Planetoid X16 was the last port of call and MacGregor was inclined to think that a demob 'happy' mood – 'end of term' – had gripped the crew. Hans, the Dutch biologist, had taken to singing in the shower. A trial to all and a sure sign that his thoughts were far from the wavelength of scientific exploration. Perhaps they'd all grown a little careless. Preoccupied. Not surprising given the time away from home. Long past the time when a crew – even a crew like his which had spent several tours of duty together – became tetchy and fractious. Seeing the same old faces day after day, week after week. Now, month after month! Psychological tests, compatibility assessments, endless acclimatisation training, past familiarity. MacGregor smiled wryly and, of course, planet X16 hadn't helped. A real anticlimax—little more than a large lump of rock, apparently totally devoid of animal life and with practically no flora.

"Some bureaucrat of the Ministry between cups of tea and digestives thought up this little treat!" Jim, the chief engineer, had a jaundiced view of the chair-bound element of the Space Ministry.

So it wasn't exactly a connected, well-motivated group who clambered down from the space capsule onto the rocky surface of planetoid X16. Above, the ship gleamed in the sunlight. *A little weather-worn,* thought MacGregor, *definitely in need of a car wash. Perhaps we all are.*

The atmosphere was borderline tolerable-high oxygen content, a little surprising in this removed quadrant of the galaxy.

And that's the only surprise, thought MacGregor,

glancing at the barren desolation all around.

"Hope we didn't forget the deckchairs," said Jim.

Alan, the geologist, had a more succinct comment.

"What a godforsaken spot!"

"I shouldn't think he was ever here in the first place," commented Jim.

Most saw his point. All around, rocks, dust, debris, distant glimpses of rocky outcrops—and a surprisingly thick soil.

"John Innes No. 2," said Hans approvingly.

"My chrysanthemums would do well in this," added Jim. A double life one wouldn't have suspected.

No sight or sound of animal or even insect life. That was partly a relief. It reduced the workload. The sooner the chores were over—the sooner home. What there was – was the plant. The plant because despite the John Innes No. 2, it appeared to be the only one. Surprisingly robust, on average about four feet tall, a sturdy stalk topped by a bulbous head with a coronet of orange leaves. Hans had bent down and looked intently at the 'head' of one of the plants.

"If this thing had eyes and a mouth I could talk to it."

The crew stood about rather listlessly, chatting. There seemed no motivation—an apparent general reluctance to settle down for the business at hand. MacGregor felt some of the negativity in himself. It took a deliberate effort of will to shake off the mood.

"You people going to take root. Let's get on with it."

The unusual sharpness in MacGregor's customary measured tone was noted with some surprise. However, the crew members stirred and moved to take up their usual tasks.

Two parties went out to survey. MacGregor led one, Jim the other. Hans and his assistant turned to extracting several of the plants for transfer to the ship. Both survey parties stumbled rather aimlessly across the rock-strewn inhospitable terrain. A dry valley that conceivably could have been gouged by the fast-flowing water... once! The thought didn't muster the usual enthusiasm in MacGregor. A distant rocky outcrop. Those black patches could be caves—or not! MacGregor's mood of detachment irked him. One of his team commented in summary: "Nothing of interest."

What nagged at him was that the exact same notion, word for word, had already occurred to him. "Nothing of interest" – anywhere – even when there was "nothing of interest". His natural doggedness tracked a thing down – shook it by the scruff of the neck – until the phrase was unarguable.

"Could be something!"

MacGregor's brief reverie was fractured.

Alan, the geologist, magnifying glass in hand, was examining a small lump of grey rock.

"Shouldn't think so! Nothing of interest here!"

That damned phrase again. He was actually shocked at his negativity. He glanced apologetically at Alan but said nothing more until they reached the capsule. Jim's party was already returned. No doubt from the same desultory lethargy; entirely lacking in scientific focus. The other crew members stood idly around the capsule as if awaiting the starting pistol to board. MacGregor obliged.

"We're done here! A wasted detour!"

His own vehemence startled MacGregor and the crew. They knew the skipper as painstakingly dogged. Mr Conscientious! Sober professional competence. So, they were surprised but made no comment. All were clearly too eager to be gone. Back on his ship, MacGregor gave immediate orders for initial preparations for departure. He had a growing sense of urgency about this against which he felt obliged to after token resistance – ineffectual – as he expected. He simply couldn't account for this compulsion – this necessity – to see Planetoid X16 receding rapidly into the void.

On boarding, Alan had disappeared into his lab with his 'possibly interesting' rocks. A general relief at being back on board had relaxed the crew. Alan burst back into the control section, face flushed and alive with excitement. Exuberantly, he enthused about the mineral potential of the planet and, like a conjurer, produced the undistinguished lump of rock from a pocket.

"Of course," he said with deliberately reflective slowness, "it's only a preliminary analysis… but!"

That 'but' caught the instant attention of all. Even MacGregor brooding silently at a side table raised his head.

"But," Alan repeated, "if this is typical… *if*, I say…" a general groan of exasperated anticipation reverberated around the room.

"*If* I say…" Alan was savouring his moment in the spotlight.

"Get on with it!" shouted someone.

"If this is typical of the entire planet… then…"

15

Not total silence. Everyone expecting a favourable punchline.

"Gentlemen, welcome to Eden-vale… this place is a treasure trove! A genuine Aladdin's Cave."

The crew members in the control section, MacGregor the notable exception, were eagerly swept up by Alan's planned climax. The crew was instantly viscerally aware of the significance of Alan's words. It was intergalactic law. They – present in this control section – they – the discoveries – and they alone – not the company – would be the beneficiaries. One of the necessary inducements. To persuade young men to leave families, friends—the earth. To leave the earth for months at a time to go wandering among lumps of rock in remote parts of the galaxy. Each man in that control section had read the small print in their contracts. Knew it by heart. They also knew how incredibly uncommon it was for any worthwhile exploitable mineral resources to be found. But the inducement was there, and all astronauts are dreamers after all.

"You can all stop drooling now and think seriously about how you're going to spend the bonanza."

As usual, Jim got in first:

"I'm going to buy the Space Ministry building and bulldoze it to the ground."

A general cheer greeted this. MacGregor hung back. He felt a quite acute reluctance to join in the celebrations. He shouted above the din.

"Calm down everybody! Let's get this ship off this planet and home!"

"That's right," agreed Alan, "the sooner we're off

16

this godforsaken hole, the sooner we're home and the sooner the developers can move in. Welcome to the modern world X16. You beaut! A golden globe – solid gold – hanging in space. I can see that endless tsunami of royalty cheques rolling in."

Wholehearted enthusiasm met this sentiment. MacGregor sat sombre and slightly apart from the rest. His vision of the future was quite different. He imagined the desolate surface of X16 covered with equipment of all sizes and shapes; vast excavations in progress; endless armies of workers engaged in a multitude of tasks; mammoth cargo ships arriving and leaving; a pall of flames mantling the planet; the racket constant, the piles of discarded refuse and equipment—a galactic dustbin. He shuddered. He felt a sense of deep, aching sadness. A profound sorrow for the fate of X16. A vision of hell.

"Come on, Skipper!"

The cry, seeming distant and vague, hardly penetrated MacGregor's self-absorption. His introspection had reached a critical point. A sudden conviction, an indignation, that the basics of his self-belief, anchored in his solid sense of professional competence, was being threatened—undermined. Why? He, the seasoned most senior member of the entire crew, felt uniquely guilty, responsible in some vague sense and, for what? Surely not the fate of X16—this tiny globe of rocky desolation. A pinprick on a galactic chart. Difficult even for a practised eye to locate. In a remote sector of the 'Silent Quarter' that nobody had visited before. He didn't believe in ghosts or table-rapping either. MacGregor was only vaguely conscious of the rapturous euphoria churning around him in the Control Room. He had the sense that he was being made a fool of—the victim of some psychological practical joke. Withoutan explanation or reason, was that it?! If so, why just now? He wasn't the imaginative type. The mere thought amused him. Other crew members, even the 'men of science' qualified as, at least, part-time 'dreamers'. Not Hamish MacGregor. No! Whatever the culprit – his emotions were not the problem, these were well-disciplined – always obedient – always well-marshalled, unless, and this thought really rattled him, they were being manipulated? Was he, somehow, being used? The thought raised the obvious questions, by whom, or what, and why?

"Skipper! Skipper!"

"Must be dreaming about the money!"

Two crew members yanked MacGregor out of his reverie and out of his seat. Someone had suddenly remembered that Hans wasn't there.

MacGregor, mind still preoccupied with the questions by whom? or what? and why? was processed with the festiveminded crowd along the corridor towards the laboratory.

The door of the laboratory glided open. The crowd stopped abruptly. The set seven specimens of Planetoid X16's sole example of flora were planted, in their own soil, in a line along the edge of the room. Hans sat on a low stool facing the middle plant. The heads of the three plants on either side of the central one seemed to be turned towards Hans, though that might have been an impression due to perspective and the subdued light. The striking thing was Hans. Sitting on the edge of the stool, hands on knees, head thrust forward staring directly at the bland head of the middle plant directly in front of him. Hans' head was not more than a foot from the plant. The entire impression was of a deep and earnest conversation in progress—but a conversation without words.

The atmosphere of gleeful euphoria that had filled the corridor a moment before had stopped as if a switch had been flicked. MacGregor was the first to react. He first glanced at the faces nearest to him. No other way to describe it. A look of awareness of comprehension was unmistakable. MacGregor motioned the crew to stay at the door while he moved silently across the room to stand behind Hans. Without speaking he laid a hand on Hans' shoulder. There was enough light in the lab to see Hans' pale face, eyes moist with tears. MacGregor nodded to him and said:

"I know! They've got to go back."

MacGregor now knew without further explanation the answer to all his questions.

"And now!" Hans added urgently.

MacGregor glanced at the silent faces at the lab door. He had his answers about them wrenched from an opulent vision of a luxurious future. As they had expected, the euphoric mood had drained out of them. Even Jim, with a set, intent gaze, was a million wisecracking miles from the 'treasure-hunting' moments of a few, a few? Aeons-long moments ago.

The silent row of plants now seemed to have turned towards the men at the door about to leave.

Later, with the essential task completed, the crew

assembled in the Control Room. MacGregor sat before the computer console. It was a procedural formality, on completion of a mission, to send a brief preliminary report to the Ministry. A fuller report would follow on arrival at base. Unless, of course, something extraordinary necessitated extraordinary measures. A sort of snap judgement on Planetoid X16.

Unusually, for this routine task, MacGregor had an audience—in fact, the entire crew. They were packed uncomfortably in the cramped space, straining to see the screen. *As though,* thought MacGregor idly, *they want to make sure I get it right.*

"From: Captain Hamish MacGregor – Galactic ship Odyssey II.

To: Space Ministry, London.

Subject: Preliminary Report – Planetoid X16 sector AQ14B16."

MacGregor's reports were invariably a model of concision—a talent much appreciated by hard-pressed report-reading staff at the Ministry.

"Devoid of all flora and fauna. Barren. Inhospitable. No commercial potential."

MacGregor added his final comment.

"Nothing of interest."

An Unexpected Adventure in the Department Store

"N'Komo! N'Komo!" Mr Parkinson's voice roared through the salaries and costing department of the Kenyan Copper Company. Between the double row of desks, N'Komo shuffled towards the office of the departmental head.

One of the African clerks looked up as he went by. "Hurry up N'Komo or you'll get the sack!" All the large expanses of smiling faces from the nearby desks joined in the chorus of laughter. The anxious lines around N'Komo's eyes deepened and he increased speed. His age was indeterminate. He had worked for the company since the salaries department had been housed in a corrugated iron hut.

"Take all that rubbish out!" commanded Mr Parkinson when N'Komo appeared at the glass-panelled door. He pointed to a heap of papers on the desk.

"Yes, Mr Parkinson!" This was N'Komo's invariable reply.

The simple abbreviation of 'sir' had never seemed appropiate tfor him.

"There's a very important man coming this afternoon and

I want this office looking neat and tidy. Understand, N'Komo?"

"Yes, Mr Parkinson."

N'Komo was occupied all the morning on his task. He was used to the laughter of the salary clerks as he bustled about the office. But there seemed much more of it that day. The clerks were in an excited and rather mystified mood. Mr Parkinson had told them that the chairman of the company was coming from Nairobi just to talk to them. It was an important occasion. They knew the chairman's name – it cropped up on a lot of correspondence they dealt with – but they had never seen him before. Mr Parkinson had given no hint about the reason for the visit.

N'Komo sat under the shade of a small shrub. This was the dry season and the brown bush landscape stretched away before him. As a young man, many years before, he had crossed the bush alone and on foot. It was then that he had first worked for the Kenyan Copper Company. Each year since, he had watched new buildings go up and more people arrive. It still seemed a miracle to him. Only three days' journey away by foot his own people were scratching a hard living from the soil. Yet here in dry and arid desert country everyone was happy and affluent .

N'Komo sat on and dreamed away the long break in the middle of the day. There was a sudden chatter of voices. N'Komo looked up and saw all the fineshirted clerks of the salaries and costing department leaning through the office windows talking excitedly and pointing. A large gleaming car was coming up the road between the mine area and the administrators' block. The clerks vanished from the windows as the car stopped at the entrance.

Mr Parkinson was the most important person in N'Komo's world. He couldn't grasp the idea that anyone was more important than him.

N'Komo stood up and shuffled back towards the office. Mr Parkinson had told him that he could have the afternoon off; that he wouldn't be wanted. But N'Komo now knew clearly that he wanted to see the this important man who had come in the big expensive car.

The office door of the costing department had a small square window in it. N'Komo saw that all the bright white shirts were gathered down at the far end of the office. A stranger was standing on a chair talking to them. N'Komo stared in amazement. It could be possible that this was the great man. He was very short and round with a bald head and perspiring face. Mr Parkinson's huge gaunt frame towered beside him.

"... so, unfortunately, we have had to arrive at the conclusion that economies are necessary. There is no other way of meeting the increased costs." The voice was hard and bright, jabbing out like a spear. N'Komo listened out of habit but understood nothing of what went on. Until, at length, the small, round man said: "The computer will be here next Monday. Most of you, I'm afraid, will be made redundant. I've been discussing the matter with Mr Parkinson and we think that 30 of the 32 of you employed here will have to leave. We have arranged generous compensation terms."

A general hubbub of conversation broke out in the room. N'Komo understood that 30 of the superior white-shirted clerks were to be replaced by a single man called a computer. He must be a wonderful man, thought N'Komo. Far greater than Mr Parkinson and the little man standing on the chair.

On the following Monday morning, N'Komo was ordered to clear the desks from the office into the storeroom. Only two were left in the large, empty room. The two young Africans sitting at them felt very proud that they had been selected to work with the new computer.

At about 11 o'clock a lorry arrived, and two men carried a wooden crate into the office and set it down near Mr Parkinson's door. N'Komo's lined face was a picture of surprise. He had expected the new computer man to arrive in a large shining car—even larger than the chairman's. Yet here he was in a wooden box.

Perhaps he couldn't walk, thought N'Komo.

Mr Parkinson had recently been in London on a computer training course. He eagerly but carefully removed the packaging from around the computer. At last, it stood with its back to the wall boldly facing the empty office. It was about four feet tall and six feet long.

N'Komo stood in front of it, puzzled. It was only a box, and it didn't move. It looked completely dead.

"All right," said Mr Parkinson to the remaining clerks, "we'll have a trial run". He plugged in the current and made rapid adjustments to switches and knobs.

The computer twitched and chattered into life. It winked at N'Komo with six eyes: blue, red and green. It spoke in a loud humming voice which N'Komo couldn't understand.

It eats paper, thought N'Komo, as he saw Mr Parkinson feeding the punched computer card into its mouth. *That's what it doesn't want,* he thought, as the narrow strip of paper emerged from a different part.

"Works fine!" said Mr Parkinson to his assistants. "It shouldn't take us more than a morning to do the work it took all 32 of you a whole week to complete." Mr Parkinson laughed as he saw their astonished faces. The company planned to make Mr Parkinson's unit a sort of calculations headquarters, to which work would be sent from various places.

N'Komo squatted on the floor and gazed at the computer. "The computer man must be very great!" he muttered over and over to himself.

The next morning, Mr Parkinson arrived at his office early. He was eager to play with his new toy. Stacked neatly beside the data-feed-in area of the computer was a pile of paper. Mr Parkinson bent down to examine it. There were old newspapers, sugar bags, flour bags, paper of every size and age.

"N'Komo!" bellowed Mr Parkinson, in a menacing voice. But N'Komo did not come, either then or later.

Computer operations had proceeded smoothly for about a week. Mr Parkinson was delighted. The two clerks were quite happy—there was far less work to do than under the old arrangement.

On the Monday following the arrival of the computer, Mr Parkinson walked back towards his office after lunch, whistling happily. A very friendly phone call from the chairman that morning had boosted his spirits. It had been hinted broadly that as the man in charge of what would eventually become the most rapidly expanding section of the company he could expect 'great things' if everything went as planned.

Why shouldn't they? he thought.

Three dust-covered staff were squatting in front of the computer as he entered.

N'Komo was standing beside the computer with a scruffy bundle in his hands.

"What the hell is all this about?" yelled Mr Parkinson. "What the devil do you think this is, a bloody sideshow?!"

The three Africans stood up raising a cloud of dust as they turned round. N'Komo carefully placed the bundle on the floor near the computer and approached Mr Parkinson.

"Outside, all of you!" Mr Parkinson was trembling with anger. He pointed to the door to make his meaning quite clear.

With his ageless head bowed, N'Komo began to speak: "Mr Parkinson…"

Parkinson cut him short. "Get them out! And you've got the sack! This is a business. You can't just wander off for a week without a word to anyone."

N'Komo glanced anxiously back at the computer and then trailed through the door followed by the three blanketed Africans. Mr Parkinson picked up the dirty bundle of scrap paper which N'Komo had left and threw it into a waste bin.

All that afternoon, he felt uneasy. Concentration eluded him and, in the end, he switched off the computer and called it a day. From his window, he could see N'Komo and the other staff sitting in the shade of shrub, staring steadily at the building. *What the hell did they want,* he thought? He nearly telephoned the security office to have them removed but decided that might make him look a fool.

By Wednesday morning the crowd of Africans clustered around the administration building numbered over 500. More were appearing hourly. Coming tirelessly out of the dusty scrubland in two and three or larger groups. There was no noise or disturbance—all sat quietly staring at the building. N'Komo seemed to be the acknowledged leader. From time to time he stood up and moved among the seated Africans, talking and pointing to the administration building. Mr Parkinson was in a state of restrained desperation. The small security staff were quite helpless against the numbers there.

On Friday morning, a crisis point had been reached. A vast encampment of local people spilled over the entire workings of the Kenyan Copper Company and the countryside around. The focal point was the administration building and N'Komo. Operations at the mine had ceased the day before and any kind of mechanised movement from one part of the working to another was impossible. In the afternoon, the chairman, perspiring freely, walked through the silent mass to the administration building and Mr Parkinson. N'Komo was summoned urgently by Mr Parkinson.

"We want computer-man to help," he said to that baffled red-faced chairman. "Computer-man is a great man! He can do work of 30 people in one morning. I went home to my tribe and told them. So they all come here. We all bring food, Mr Parkinson! Everyone brought paper for the computer-man to eat."

Mr Parkinson knew the hard, precarious existence most of the crowd assembled outside lived. He considered himself a shrewd handler of native labour, but he felt greatly moved.

N'Komo made it clear that they intended to stay until computer-man helped them.

The computer was removed on the Monday, two weeks to the day since it had arrived. Before midday, the multitude had evaporated into the bush. N'Komo was reinstated but his faith in the computer-man was shattered. He could not understand why he should have gone when there was so much to do. The only compensation was the favoured treatment he received from the 30 clerks who were back working in the salaries and costing department.

The October 3rd Tale

The Chamber of Commerce lunch was dull. Why the
devil they pick these so-called experts to come and talk
to us I don't know. Outsiders who couldn't tell a pick
from a bulldozer. At any rate, Bill Jones and Clyde
Overton were sitting next to me. The food had been good,
and we had to talk about something while the idiot ranted
on. Bill asked for the old story again, said Clyde hadn't
heard it. Well, it's no great hardship to make yourself out
a hero, so I began again.

It was Tuesday, October 3rd, last year. I left home in
Hampstead very early that day. As you know, I'm a
contractor; one of the biggest and all built up in 10 years.
There was a conference in Manchester about one of the
motorway contracts up in the North-West. We got it you
remember, and damned good business it was. Anyway, I
don't like flying so I drove up.

It was a hard day's work but that's how I like 'em. I
finally got back home about nine o'clock. The house was
completely dark. This was strange because May, my wife,
isn't one for the gay social life; neither am I. We don't go
out much and when we do, it's nearly always together.
When I got in I called out, no answer. I went into the

kitchen and found the remains of breakfast on the table just as I'd left them in the morning. Well, you can imagine how I felt. It's a damned funny experience, something like that; unnerving. I went upstairs and there was no sign of her.

After a bit, I just sat down and tried to think. Do you know one possibility that just never occurred to me? That May might have left me. As you can see, I'm no Romeo. I'm only 45 but I'm prepared to admit I look a damned sight older. You don't build up a business like mine from scratch in 10 years without showing the scars. May's a good bit younger than I am and a fine woman; not just in looks, in every way.

Anyway, after a while, I realised I'd have to phone the police. Before they arrived, I heard a faint knocking in the kitchen. It came from a broom cupboard in there. When I opened the door, my god what a sight! May was inside—tied up like a bloody chicken! And gagged too! She was only half-conscious. I carried her into the lounge and gave her some brandy to drink. At first, she was far too dazed or shocked to say anything much. She first lay there on the settee with her eyelids flickering. Then all of a sudden she seemed to come round, and she broke down. My God, if the characters who'd done it had walked into the room I'd have murdered them there and then.

It was quite a while before May could speak. Just as the police arrived at the door she managed to say:

"They said they haven't finished with you yet!"

Just like that, it turned out to be Inspector Brown of the local force who came round. We play golf together and he thought he'd give me the personal treatment.

Anyway, he suggested calling the doctor. I was so upset and furious it just hadn't occurred to me. The doctor said May should go to bed, she was suffering from shock.

Inspector Brown asked me if I'd any idea what might have happened but, of course, I hadn't. I even went as far as saying that if he ever found out who did it I'd appreciate five minutes alone with them, as a personal favour. He suggested robbery. I said there were no signs of it, but he asked me to check.

Everything seemed in order until I checked the safe; it's behind a bookcase in the lounge. It looked all right but Inspector Brown asked me to open it. Now I always keep a fair amount of cash in the house apart from May's jewellery. Every damned thing was gone: private letters, papers and all. There must have been £30,000 worth of stuff.

Before the doctor could give May a sedative, she insisted on telling Inspector Brown and me the story. It seems she's stayed at breakfast reading the papers after I'd gone. About half an hour later, she answered the doorbell. Two men with stockings over their heads pushed in. They asked where I was; May said I was out. They obviously didn't believe her because one of the men took a gun out of his pocket and searched the house. May said that the taller of the two seemed furious. The other one was all for leaving, but then, the tall one asked where the safe was. At first, May wouldn't tell him but then he said something about waiting until I got back. Hell, I wish he had! So they emptied the safe and then put May in the kitchen cupboard. And there she stayed all day until I got back. The doctor said if the gag had been tighter she could easily have suffocated.

Inspector Brown seemed to think I was in some sort of danger. I didn't agree. I told him they were two bloody cowardly ruffians who liked bullying defenceless women. Inspector Brown's a stubborn man once he gets hold of an idea. Anyway, he said that from May's story it seemed likely that the robbery was an afterthought, and I was their main objective. I told him that May was in such a state that she was probably confused about exactly what had happened and what was said. But I made it damned clear that if he didn't catch those so-and-so's I'd spend some of my own money until I did.

The next day, of course, we had the press crawling all over the house. I pity the poor devils who have to endure publicity like that all the time. May was much better by then and she spent the whole of the following morning cutting out the news items and photographs from all the papers. Inspector Brown had no news, so I went to the office as usual.

Mrs Cleaver (page 5, line 14), my secretary, said a man had waited some time to see me but he'd left. He hadn't left a name. I didn't think anything about it until I noticed one of the morning papers on a chair. There was a photograph of May and me on the front page. My face had been ringed with a red pencil and crossed out. Mrs Cleaver (page 5, line 19) said the man had been tall and slender. She thought she would recognise him again. I can tell you I felt relieved. I felt that we had the bastard—too sure of himself by half. I left the office intending to go straight to the police. When I got into the car, he was there. He must have been hiding in the back seat. The devil had a gun, but I saw red and went for him. Anyway, he knocked me out and when I came round his friend was in the car as well, driving. The tall fellow was still in the back seat, he stuck his gun in my neck. I turned round to get a good look at him. Whatever happened I wasn't going to forget his face again! The little runt who was driving seemed as nervous as hell.

"So we meet at last," the tall fellow said to me.

I told him that I'd see him in gaol for 10 years before the day was out. "You'll be dead long before then, Mr Contractor Beddow," he said.

He looked half crazy to me, and I was damned sure he meant what he said.

"You killed my father, Beddow. That's a debt you're going to pay today," he added. I told him he was a raving lunatic and that he'd better let me go there and then.

He went on about having waited a long time for this chance.

I could see we were driving somewhere near the docks. After a while, we turned into a small alley between two warehouses. We got out underneath a fire escape which ran up to the top of one of the buildings. The place was completely deserted.

"You remember how he died, Beddow? Suicide they called it; from the roof," the fellow said.

I tried to barge into him to see if I could knock the gun out of his hand, but he was too quick. That's where I got this scar across the cheek. There was nothing else to do so we started climbing up the fire escape. I went first and the small fellow came up at the back.

Now, I knew the chap was mad. It wouldn't do the slightest good to try to talk to him. And after what he'd done to May, I didn't feel like trying. My chance came near the top. I'd turned onto the last flight of steps and he was on the flight below. I swung round and lashed out with my foot. I caught him in the chest, and he simply fell back and went straight over the rail. His gun dropped onto the landing. The little fellow looked scared out of his wits. He just turned and ran off.

Well, that's about it. The police found a few notes about me in the fellow's pockets. My name, address and suchlike. They put him down as a crackpot. Inspector Brown says they come across people like that now and again. They take a dislike to somebody who's successful and then invent some sort of grievance against them. They never found the little fellow though. But he wasn't the real bastard—that was the other chap.

As usual, the story went down very well. It never fails. Clyde even made some crack about 'real James Bond stuff'. By God! I'd like to see his face if he knew the truth. I still wonder though, how Young found out that I killed his father.

The Fifty Pound Note

Monday morning. Mrs Lambert was at the altar straightening the cloth and removing the remains of a derelictooking bunch of chrysanthemums from a chipped glass vase. She glanced around the gloomy interior of the deserted church. Her mind flicking back to the time she and Jack had sat in the second-row pew. A church – a large church – more than half full. Any Sunday. Special occasions overflowing. A lovely but subdued buzz of multiple conversations awaiting the arrival of the vicar.

That was the time of Mr Spencer. Already in his 70s—after nearly 40 years in the parish. He had seen his congregation dwindle year by year. A steady unchecked rate of natural wastage that seemed to syphon the lifeblood out of his vocation. Yet, Mr Spencer liked to assert, there were many churches that wouldn't muster a congregation like his. Mrs Lambert remembered him lead off the hymn singing with a brave, marginally, tuneless fortissimo. Mrs Lambert and Albert had thoroughly enjoyed the vigorous singing and the warmth of a sense of communal identity.

The sound of the heavy outer door creaking open scattered the memories. "Still here, Emily?"

Mr Coleman was the new vicar. New in the sense of recent – only just over a year – and new in the sense of freshness. A crisp, sympathetic young man. Eager, devout – undoubtedly – but also, Mrs Lambert thought, with a quality not always present in the young – a natural empathy for people – aware of their feelings and genuinely, not professionally, caring. Mrs Lambert was of an age to feel that empathy was a quality for older, if not old, people. Rare, usually non-existent, in the self-obsession of youth. At least that was what she thought until she had met Mr Coleman. She felt – she knew – he had brought his natural compassion into the church not, simply acquired it, like a vestment, as a mark of his vocation. To question in the past year, he had broadened her view of the positive possibilities of human nature. She had even grown to approve of his habit of cycling about in jeans and pullover without dog collar.

"How did we do yesterday, Emily?"

Mr Coleman dreaded asking the question.

"Then why do you ask it?" his wife often said to him with a smile.

"Because, darling, I have to, Mrs Lambert expects it."

He knew every time from the anguish in her face how much the inevitable answer caused a deep and genuine pain. He tried to lighten the atmosphere by making the necessity a sort of standing joke between them.

"Can we still afford the communion wine?"

It had been one of Mrs Lambert's self-appointed chores – since well before the appointment of Mr Coleman – to count the Sunday collection. Even in the short time he had been there, the number of coins had dwindled, the occasional notes had become fewer, and the total amount would have been dispiriting to a less favourable temperament than Mr Coleman's.

In one sense Mrs Lambert's concern was well-founded. She had inspected the moth-eaten, the decaying, possibly dangerous masonry, listened sadly to the occasionally asthmatic wheeze of the organ. No matter where she looked, the unspoken need for money, for investment, for renewal. Mr Coleman already had pastoral responsibility for a group of three churches – in varying states of debility. He cycled between the three churches on a rota basis – the churches' funds certainly wouldn't run to the upkeep of a car.

But who these days wanted to invest their money in churches? Mrs Lambert was well aware that life was difficult for many people; churchgoing a low priority and the thought of actually giving to the church not even on the list.

"As usual, Mr Coleman. Poorly! Down on last week and last week was a really low point!"

"Let's not despair, Emily. The good Lord will provide."

It was a natural formula and Mr Coleman felt rather guilty that he had resorted to it. Mrs Lambert gave the ghost of a grateful smile but, he thought, quite unconvinced.

She suddenly burst out as though releasing pent-up emotion.

"What we need Mr Coleman is a sign that he is aware of

our problem. That he knows!"

Mr Coleman now glimpsed an inner desolation in Mrs Lambert—previously only a sort of settled despondency.

He was troubled because he couldn't understand why she felt this way. To him the church was people. Real people—the ones he met daily as he went around the town, and the outer villages that comprised his geographically extended parish. He met people with hopes, despairs… optimistic, fearful. Human nature in fact. People he related and responded to and to whom he believed, though he never attempted the mental tally himself, his natural cheerfulness and empathy was welcome. Of course, the church stuff was a responsibility. A heritage. Twelfth-century in origin. The physical embodiment of a long tradition of worship. But still an inanimate combination of stone, wood and glass. An uncomfortable one. He thought wryly of his first winter preaching to a cold echoing cavernous space with dim lighting to 20 shivering people. Even a robust optimism couldn't be unaffected. But, still, to him the primary concern was the entire community of souls—churchgoers or not, old and young, ill or healthy, honest or not, believing in whatever. That was his mission—those were his priorities.

Crumbling masonry, loose painting, a leaky roof, poor lighting, of course he was aware—he saw them every day. With unlimited resources, of course, improvement would be made. They didn't loom large on Mr Coleman's moral landscape. The five couldn't understand how this concern for the mere fabric of a building – even a church – had become so enmeshed in Mrs Lambert's emotional, and, as he saw it, physical wellbeing. But it had. The anguish was there in front of him and the danger.

"It's almost as if God has deserted us."

"Oh, come, Emily."

He wanted to say *it's only a building*. Obviously, that wouldn't help.

"I'm sorry Mrs Lambert, I didn't quite mean that – I know it's unchristian in a way, but I really think he should give us some sign that he cares about this beautiful church. It is his spiritual home – and ours."

Mr Coleman followed her tearful gaze around the church. Gloomy even on a bright day. Great wells of darkness stretching up to the barely glimpsed timber roof. Mr Coleman simply didn't know how to reply to her.

Mrs Lambert didn't seem to expect a reply. She turned and began clearing away some fallen chrysanthemum leaves from the altar cloth.

Mr Coleman with an untypically hopeless shrug of the shoulders made his way to the door. There he paused and looked back. Mrs Lambert was only of medium height with a very spare figure but now, to the vicar, as he looked, she seemed somehow diminished. Shrunken. She looked vulnerable. Mr Coleman was shocked. He also felt something that was quite new, and unwelcome, in his new ministry. Hopelessness.

Mrs Lambert wasn't simply a member of the church she was a friend, and, as usual, Mr Coleman discussed matters with his wife. Sylvia was bright, pragmatic, confident in her own judgement. This self-reliance made her a great believer in individual responsibility. Destiny or fate was just an excuse. So it wasn't a surprise when his wife's initial response was: "It's an obsession. I like Mrs Lambert, but old folk do get these quirks. She'll get over it!"

"How did I marry an agnostic?"

"You mean apart from my teacher's salary to boost your stipend, mainly, because you wanted to convert me. Put me on the straight and narrow."

They both laughed. Sylvia put her arms about him and looked earnestly into his face.

"You can't worry about everybody. People have got to do things for themselves. Mrs Lambert will get over it."

Mr Coleman kissed his wife and gently remonstrated, "No, she won't! Not all people are like you darling—some need help to… 'get over it'. But, how, how?"

"I'll get you a large whisky!"

Sylvia was a confirmed believer in the restorative power of a matured whisky. Mr Coleman swivelled in his chair. He was only too conscious of the urgency of the problem; the situation seemed unanswerable. The mysterious crock of gold under the old oak in the churchyard. Finding a previously well-concealed benefactor among the meagre congregation. Miracles were rare—at least in pounds sterling or in any currency. No, if there was a solution more than a reassuring confiding presence, Mr Coleman thought it would have to be something simple!

That's the type of thing that would appeal to Mrs Lambert. But…?

Sylvia reappeared with the whisky. She didn't believe in the saviour of souls drinking alone. Fortified, Mr Coleman turned back to the desk to continue composing the Sunday sermon, 'The Good Samaritan'. 'The Good Samaritan'. The theme oddly merged with his previous thought of a simple solution to generate an idea. Not a miracle. Not a windfall. Simple but, to Mrs Lambert, he hoped persuasive.

"Sylvia! Have you ever seen a £50 note?"

His wife was in the midst of her second major swallow of whisky and almost choked.

The wait till the next Sunday was nerve-wracking. Sylvia, of course, explained about good money being wasted on a crackpot idea. Mr Coleman had thanked her for that judgement. The vicar's active involvement in varied community work kept him occupied and thankfully preoccupied. But the thought nagged. He did have doubts about his bright idea. Simple – yes – but – simplistic.

Mrs Lambert was not naive – let alone simple-minded.

On Sunday, Mr Coleman entered the church, peered round the door expecting to see Mrs Lambert busy at the altar as usual. No—the opening door almost caught Mrs Lambert in the face. A face wholly transformed from the previous week. Was it hope—or as Sylvia said later that Mrs Lambert had probably had that second egg for

41

breakfast? There was no mistaking the excited glow of satisfaction in Mrs Lambert's eyes.

"The sign, Mr Coleman!"

Trying to sound innocent of any prior knowledge, Mr Coleman said: "Oh! A good week, Emily?"

"Look!"

She produced the £50 note from her pocket like a stage magician. The vicar kept up his prepared strategy.

"Very welcome, of course, but it doesn't transform church funds, Emily."

"You miss the point, Mr Coleman. I know the congregation – all of them – there's not one that could afford that—certainly not to put in a church collection."

The vicar felt a little guilty now by deception—only a little guilty. "I don't see what you mean…"

"Don't you see, Mr Coleman? He works in mysterious ways. It's not the amount. He heard. He was here. He's listened. He touched somebody's heart, so they made the gesture."

"Oh, I see!" said Mr Coleman.

Best thing is not to tell Sylvia that probably £20 would have been enough.

The Horoscope

Emily Carter had not felt so uncomfortable and so unsure of her emotional bearings for… well, forever. The stability of her marriage had never been in question—had never given her a moment's anxiety. She loved Phil dearly and was quite certain he felt the same. She had always had complete confidence in him—and confidence is not measured by percentages. One can't have, say, 65% confidence in one's spouse or in anybody! It's either there or it isn't! These were articles of faith with Emily, or had been, until three days ago. Now, such psychological self-reassurance seemed unconvincing. Emily fidgeted in her lounge chair staring distractedly into her third cup of coffee. She hated to be inactive and now at 10 o'clock, the morning was half gone, and nothing was done. Her mental – 'things to do' – list still had all its boxes unticked – including the critical one – 'ask Phil about it!' That had been the obvious thing to do—and she hadn't done it! Then her disquiet wasn't in any way soothed by Anne Sparling's phone call.

"Well, yesterday afternoon in town I saw Phil with a very… attractive… young woman!" Anne underlined these words with heavy emphasis as though to avoid the fact that Emily might miss the point.

"They were walking by the river. I was on the other

side. I waved and Phil didn't respond. He seemed very… involved! Even from a distance, you can tell these things!"

The keywords got the same emphatic treatment. Emily felt a strong urge to demand, bluntly, what Anne was implying.

"I only rang because I know Phil normally plays golf on Thursday afternoons?"

The question mark was obvious—though Anne made it sound more like an accusation than a question. Emily remained silent. Anne went on.

"I hope you don't mind me calling, Emily… I thought you should know!"

"Yes, Phil did mention it to me but thank you anyway, Anne. Bye!"

With that white lie, Emily rang off, abruptly. There was just a chance it might slow the headlong torrent of Anne's gossip.

She wasn't hopeful. In a small village like hers, scandal moved faster than a scalded cat. Real or imagined, it didn't matter. If it had any legs at all, it ran. Emily didn't much relish the thought of being its latest victim. But her main anxiety was the mounting tension that has been troubling her now for some days – before the phone call – and even before the other incidents. Her whole life Emily had possessed a sort of sixth sense – an intuition, an unsettling feeling would grip her from time to time – the uneasy sense that something was going to happen. If it were a gift – as one of her friends called it – it wasn't a comfortable one. The real biting uncertainty was that she rarely had any real focus on what the 'something' was. It was rather like the hair standing up on the back of your neck—but not being able to spot the cause.

"You're a dreamer, Emily!"

Her mother had said to her many times when she was a child. And, of course, she was—but then to some extent, most children normally are. Emily always knew the difference between dreaming and reality. That some things were real – others imaginary – and that there was a definite boundary between the two. Until she was nine she had a friend – a koala bear – Kiki – and naturally, they had conversations – she spoke to him – he spoke to her – and, naturally, he was imaginary. More real to her than many 'real things'—but still imaginary. And naturally, he never said a word to her mother. He never sat at the table with them, never went to school with her. How could he? He was imaginary. Emily Carter, the grown-up, the ex-teacher of 52, married to Phil the accountant for 22 years, was not a dreamer. She didn't read tea leaves, gaze into a crystal ball, or read palms. She didn't know the future, couldn't predict it. She was not a clairvoyant! Emily saw herself as an intelligent woman who appreciated that there were influences, vibes if you like, that some people were sensitive to, and most people weren't. It wasn't magic, it was just a fact. Very often a troubling, very disconcerting fact. Like the time two years before when she refused point-blank to go into the greenhouse and wouldn't let Phil go in. It was dangerous! She had an utter conviction about that. But beyond that, she couldn't say what the danger was – or when it would happen – but something would happen, that she was certain of. One

45

week later it did! An articulated lorry loaded with heavy steel pipes had tried to corner at speed, crashed through their garden wall and demolished the greenhouse.

Another time she had anticipated by 24 hours her daughter's call from Toronto announcing the pregnancy. So, these events – sensed but only vaguely foreseen – could be sometimes welcome but sometimes not.

So, there were the two previous startling events – now Anne's phone call – all reinforcing Emily's unsettling intuition of some imminent threat. But threat to what—to herself, to Phil, to her marriage? That was the point, she hardly ever knew, until it happened!

First, there was the passport, two days ago! It seemed much much longer. Emily had often felt that her more disturbing intuitions could stretch minutes into hours—hours into days.

Emily had called at the dry cleaners to collect her coat and Phil's suit. The man behind the counter had produced the passport.

"Lucky this fell out of the pocket before the suit went into the machine!"

Emily had thought little about it—except to wonder why Phil's passport was in his pocket. It was only when she was putting the suit away in the wardrobe that she examined it.

Phil had renewed his passport and said nothing to her. This was unusual, so was her reaction. Normally she would simply have asked him why. But she hadn't! Then the second incident.

Phil had gone for a usual weekly round of golf with Jack Renton. The Rentons were good friends who lived in the neighbouring village. Phil was very late for the evening meal, so she had phoned Jack to find out if Phil had left the club on time. Phil hadn't played golf that day. Emily had made some apology about having forgotten.

"Sorry I'm late darling. The course was crowded— very slow."

And that was it! Emily recalled watching Phil's expression as he told her the barefaced lie. His manner was calm, unruffled, in fact as near chirpy as someone of Phil's equable temperament could be. For the second time, Emily had not done the obvious thing. Have the matter out! Clear the air! Put the facts to Phil – the passport, the lie, in a matter-of-fact way – not belligerent or confrontational. Of course, Emily knew quite well why she hadn't put the question. To be candid: she was afraid! Acute anxiety about what the response could be!

Complicated by the feeling that whatever the situation it involved her as much as Phil that in questioning him, she would really be interrogating herself. No marital problem was ever 100% one-sided. And she didn't even know if there was a marital problem.

Emily took a deep draught of coffee—it was cold and repulsive, but she hardly noticed. She was thinking how destructive doubt – self-doubt, doubt of others – could be. Like water in the ground—searching and probing for any weakness with a relentless intensity then flood in with an eager destructive power. Emily shook herself—as though a vigorous movement could ward off the negative mood. She braced herself with a mental refusal to accept what had begun to seem obvious. Though the ironic thought did occur of what Mary Spanwick would have said—if

47

given the chance.

"He's going off with somebody!"

Naturally, Emily thought, she would say that. Mary was prejudiced, of course. Her husband, Frank, had run off with his secretary without any warning. However, that was Frank—and Phil was definitely not Frank. Not remotely like Frank! Emily would never claim – not that she would ever say so to anyone – that Phil's romantic moments were either frequent or earth-moving. But then again – she admitted to herself – neither were hers. Emily sincerely believed they were an excellent match. Compatible was the word. Not romantic fictions 'made in heaven' variety, but they were happy and, as important, comfortable in each other's company. They communicated. They talked—freely! Except, she thought, for the past two days. No! Emily reassured herself Phil was quite definitely not Frank! The idea had to be ridiculous! Whatever the situation was, Phil could not be in the grip of a midlife romantic flush of wanderlust. If there was one word to sum up Phil, it was 'dependable'! He was an accountant! It had always seemed the ideal profession for him. Pragmatic – systematic – 'i' dotting and 't' crossing. She always felt the profession had chosen him rather than the other way around. Emily felt a sudden acute spasm of awareness— she couldn't even think of Phil not being there. He was— necessary! Like the plumbing… the central heating. Vital! Taken for granted! You hardly knew they were there – unless – a very disturbing thought – unless something went wrong. Suddenly, Emily's efforts to reassure herself seemed pretty shaky. Again, involuntarily, she recalled what Mary would have said:

"The quiet ones! That's the sort you've got to watch! Nothing on the surface – then – when you least expect it – bang! – right between the eyes!"

With a flush of alarm, Emily suddenly perceived that Phil's – what? – difficulty? had perhaps been there – festering – in plain sight for how long? And she hadn't seen it! Wrong—not quite correct! She'd been too preoccupied to take the trouble to see it. Now she thought with some despair, even shame, of her behaviour over the past few days. In effect, she'd been spying on Phil—on her own husband. She'd been watching him – closely – furtively – every aspect of his behaviour under the microscope—'spying' had to be the word. As if he were a stranger in their own home. Anything that might trip him up—catch him out! She also felt guilty that she had not spoken out immediately. Compounding one lapse with another. Whatever happened – whatever the future – Emily felt acutely, she had not behaved in a worthy manner.

Then the post popped through the door. The horoscope had arrived. At last! She had been waiting half the morning – seeking some relief – hopefully, some pointer to a way ahead.

Though she felt the hope was pretty forlorn.

Emily Carter was not superstitious. She knew her friends mostly respected her intuition—her occasional sixth sense! But they also, mostly, ridiculed her interest in horoscopes.

"The stars, Emily! (usually accompanied by either a scornful laugh or a rueful sigh) – they come out at night

49

– that's when you dream, then you wake up and it's the real world!"

That was Debbie's favourite tack. Many times and patiently, Emily had explained that like most things in life there were good and bad. A good horoscope – prepared by someone with genuine insight – could help with a problem – a troublesome situation – or simply offer reassurance. Naturally, they were subjective and general—they had to be. Their value depended on the frame of mind you brought to them. Of course, there were no guarantees – they weren't legal documents – no 'get out of jail free' card. But, if you were open-minded? "Balderdash!"

But, at least on this subject, Debbie was not open-minded.

Emily stared through the open lounge door to where she could see the yellow wrapper of the magazine on the mat. Her mind was a war of conflicting emotions. She wanted to read the horoscope, she didn't want to; she already knew the truth, she didn't know the truth; she was afraid to find out, she wasn't afraid. No, she damned well wasn't! and with a sudden energy, she flung herself into the hall and seized the package. She tore off the wrapper and with a kind of desperation wrenched the magazine out. Then she paused! The sudden explosion of energy fizzled out—as if a switch had been flicked. The intense awareness of blame—of personal responsibility, returned. Poor Phil! The telltale signs must have been there—for how long? Taken for granted, shunted off into the emotional sidelines of her life. No wonder he… She didn't press the speculation any further. She opened the magazine and read the horoscope.

"Examine a close personal relationship—urgently! Don't delay, or permanent damage can result!"

Too late! Much too late she thought. How ironic – this horoscope was that rare thing – one that fitted the facts snugly – like a comfortable shoe. No need to twist the words – bend the meaning – fill in the gaps. This one said everything, neatly, concisely—to the point! It was all there!

At that very moment, Phil came in. His expression was serious—an air of fixed determination about him. The usual easy-going smile was absent.

"Sit down Emily. There's something I want to say!"

Emily meekly obliged with the resigned air of someone expecting – and deserving – a guilty verdict.

Phil paused. Emily was about to say she knew what he planned to do, she couldn't stop him but, he must believe she didn't want it and she was very sorry. Before she could say any of this Phil went on:

"You've probably forgotten, but you and I first met on the 8th of May, 23 years ago! Exactly! It was at the airport in Lisbon, remember? So, I've decided we're going to celebrate. An anniversary worth celebrating. Now, what do you think?"

With a mind enduring a blizzard of emotions—Emily would be quite unable to give a coherent reply, she simply nodded.

"Now this'll amuse you. You know what gave me the idea? You'd never guess! A horoscope! Yes! A horoscope! Three days ago, Jim—you know, at work, found one in a paper, somebody had left on a bus!"

Phil took a crumpled piece of paper from his pocket – laughed and said:

"Listen to this." (reads) 'Now is the moment to take the romantic initiative with someone near to you. Don't waste the chance!' "So, I didn't! I've booked the holiday! The travel agent was very helpful—a very attractive young lady by the way. Hotels, flights, all booked, and I remembered the passport. Now, I don't want any argument."

Emily had barely absorbed the news and had no intention of arguing. She wasn't even going to mention that the airport had been Faro not Lisbon—September, not May—the 28th not the 8th.

The Strange Case of Dr Carlton

Dr Carlton felt weary. Mrs Williams' latest addition was the cause of that. His evening constitutional had been delayed till well after 11. The night was moonless and starless, but the doctor strode at his usual forceful pace towards the crossroads at the bottom of Rectory Lane. After five years in the village, he knew all the local roads and paths. All the regular calls in the immediate neighbourhood of the village were made on foot. One of the *new young doctor's eccentricities*, most of the villagers thought. The term 'new doctor' infuriated Dr Carlton much more than the 'young' label.

"The way most people round here say 'new' almost implies 'barely qualified'. Presumably, you are no longer 'new' when you're deaf, half-blind, and have forgotten nine-tenths of the medicine you ever knew." Dr Carlton harped on this theme, loudly and at length in the bar of The Plough. It was not too well received by some of the other patrons.

At the crossroads, Dr Carlton halted. He felt for his cigarettes. Out of the blackness came a single piercing shriek, which was suddenly cut off. It came from the left—towards the village. Dr Carlton ran along the road. The loud echo of his feet crunching on the gravel was the only sound.

Without warning, he tripped and pitched headlong in the road. He was momentarily dazed and as he sat up the ooze of warm blood trickled down his forehead.

Then he saw the leg which had tripped him sticking out from the overgrown verge at the side of the road. It was a woman. Dr Carlton struck a match as he knelt in the thick grass.

"God!" he gasped, "Fay Parker." The pretty young face was terribly disfigured by what must have been a fearful blow on the left temple. Almost clinically, the doctor noted that there was surprisingly little blood for a gash of that extent. In the darkness, he swiftly made certain that the girl was dead. Then he squatted back on the grass.

It was almost unbelievable. Only that afternoon he had given Fay a lift back from Bracehampton. She had been shopping and was in excellent spirits.

There was a sudden cracking noise—like a twig snapping. Dr Carlton stiffened. He cocked his head to one side and listened intently. After a while, he detected a faint rustling sound. The doctor felt no fear, but a trembling anger was building up inside him. A second louder crack stabbed the darkness. Slowly, he stood up. Whoever had butchered this girl might be lurking close at hand—but where?

It was almost impossible to pinpoint a noise with any accuracy without sight.

The doctor's fury got the better of him. He leapt into the road and roared his challenge.

"Where are you? Who the devil are you? Come on, I'm

all alone; just like she was. Let's see you tackle me!"

At once, the doctor was half-blinded by the glare of powerful headlights sweeping round the corner ahead. With a harsh squeal of brakes, the car stopped. Then it reversed and with a slamming of gears raced off back along the road. Dr Carlton reached the corner as the lights of the car carving a path between the high hedges moved off.

Inspector Bancroft examined a framed diploma on the wall of the consulting room.

"I'm sorry to interrupt your surgery, Dr Carlton," he said, shambling to the cane chair usually occupied by patients.

"They can wait. They come for the gossip anyway— not to see me," Dr Carlton snapped tapping his desk impatiently with his pen.

"According to P.C. Graham, you heard someone moving near the scene of the crime?"

"The bastard was still there!"

"You know who he was?" asked the inspector keenly.

"Course not!" Dr Carlton was exasperated by police investigations. The night before, P.C. Graham, the village's time-serving law officer, had kept him waiting two hours at The Plough. Two hours, dry, in the company of Charlie Draycott, the publican, at that time of night, was no joke.

"Now, about the car, Dr Carlton," the inspector placidly went on, "did it start up near the scene of the crime or had it been moving some time when it came around that corner?"

"I don't know! I can't be sure."

The drooping walrus moustache with a suggestion of egg at one side unrigged unsatisfied. Inspector Bancroft eased his slumped body to a new position.
"Pity," he said.

"I think I recognised the car!"

"Oh!" the inspector said in surprise.
"I think it was Clarendon's jag. Simon Clarendon—the local squire. We're all supposed to doff the cap and touch the forelock."
The inspector paused and dragged at the corner of his moustache, "I believe it was rather dark last night," he said.
"If you mean how could I see," snapped Dr Carlton, "you'll remember the lights of the car. Anyway, don't take that as gospel—I only said I think I recognised the car."
"That's very useful, sir," commented the inspector. Dr Carlton glared at the slouching figure and couldn't make out whether sarcasm was intended or not.
"By the way, Dr Carlton, it was rather an odd time of night to be taking a stroll in the country!"
"You may have heard, Inspector, that doctors do not keep regular hours. If you could persuade Mrs Williams to conveniently arrange to deliver in the afternoon next time, I might get in a walk at a reasonable hour."

"The girl was dead when you got to her?"

"Yes."

"What sort of weapon would you say could cause a wound like that?"

"I don't know. I saw her for a few seconds in the light of a match. You're doing the investigating, you tell me."

"Oh! I just wondered. Every little helps, you know."

The inspector manoeuvred himself out of the chair and made for the door. "Did you know the girl well?"

The attention, the doctor noted, was on the wall. "I knew her. She was a patient."

"Was she ill?"

"Nothing serious."

Inspector Bancroft's amicable face shed some of its friendliness. He approached the desk. "What does that mean, sir?" he asked.

"It means what it says. Nothing serious. If I thought that anything I knew about the girl could be of the slightest help to you, I'd tell you. But there's nothing."

Before he finally shambled out through the door, Inspector Bancroft shot a final comment at Dr Carlton.

"If anyone was really there that night, sir, when you found the girl, I suppose he would have seen you?"

As he passed through the waiting room, the inspector noted that the sick population of Meadowvale had increased dramatically while he had been with the doctor—standing room only. And each pair of eyes, young and old, fixed on him and every tongue stilled.

"You don't have a murder every day, Constable," he said to P.C. Graham at the head of the short main street of the village. In fact, it was the only street.

P.C. Graham's stout presence was indignant at the idea. "No, sir. Bit of poaching now and again. And old Bill Waters cuts up a bit rough sometimes when he's had too much. That's all the trouble we get in Meadowvale." As guardian of this proud record of lawfulness, P.C. Graham's face flushed with pride.

"Where do the girl's parents live?" the inspector asked.

"The other side of the village. Near The Plough, sir. Not far!"

Inspector Bancroft saw that Meadowvale's curiosity wasn't limited to the doctor's waiting room. Most doorways and windows were occupied as they passed along the sunlit street.

P.C. Graham's appearance was greeted by a few 'morning John's' or at worst a curt nod.

Through his bushy eyebrows, the inspector saw the frank looks of interest or hostility were reserved for himself.

"Beg pardon for suggesting it, sir, but I think a 'foreigner' did it!"

Inspector Bancroft had been attached to Gloucestershire C.I.D. long enough to know that anyone, like himself, who didn't have at least three Meadowvale generations behind him was a 'foreigner'.

"Why?"

"You get a feeling for these things, sir. I've been village policeman here for 30 years and, of course, I was born here. I've known the people all my life—none of these could have done a thing like that!"

P.C. Graham looked pleased, as though no one could doubt that he had quite satisfactorily transferred the burden of guilt to the outside world.

"You don't have any newcomers here, then?"

"Well, not apart from the doctor. He's only been here five years come July."

P.C. Graham's disapproval was apparent.

"I suppose Dr Carlton has settled down well?"

"Well, sir, it wouldn't be my place to speak about the doctor, but – er – he is a bit difficult. People don't like him much."

"Isn't he a good doctor?"

"Oh! He's all right, I suppose. But he lives his own way. And his way isn't always ours. There's Bert Parker's place."

Just before The Plough and last in the final row on the village street was the Parkers' cottage. It was small, plain and tidy.

"Not far from where she was killed!" mused the inspector, glancing beyond the pub along the steeply hedged road leading out of Meadowvale.

Mr Parker was a huge man wearing his dark ill-fitting Sunday black. His thick wrists and gnarled fists jilted awkwardly out of the jacket sleeves as though in protest at the strange attire. Mrs Parker was a complete contrast. She was a slight woman with a drawn, refined face.

Inspector Bancroft expressed his sympathy and

accepted Mrs Parker's offer of a cup of tea.

"Could you tell me where your daughter was last night?" he asked, seated unsurely on the edge of an old horsehair sofa.

"She was in!" stated Mr Parker, standing massively by the fireplace. His wife glanced uneasily at him.

"Until what time?" the inspector gently persisted. "All night!"

Mrs Parker decided to intervene.

"At least until we went to bed, I think Bert means. We always go to bed early. Never later than half-past nine; he has to get up so early to go to the farm."

Inspector Bancroft nodded his head gratefully. As he looked up he caught a faint nod of confirmation from P.C. Graham standing by the door.

"Did she have any particular friends? Anyone she saw a great deal of?"

"Fay was a quiet girl." Mr Parker's deep, harsh voice took command again. "She helped me in the church every Sunday."

"Bert is caretaker down at the church," explained Mrs Parker, "he does it to help out."
The inspector blew noisily through the fringes of his moustache.

"Very good," he muttered, "but didn't she have any special friends? Someone she went out with? Possibly someone who called for her here?"

"I've told you, she was a good girl. She didn't want to go around wasting her time and money!"

"Did she go out of the village often?"

"She did some shopping for me in Bracehampton on

Saturday afternoons sometimes," said Mrs Parker after a cautious glance at her husband, "that was all."

"I don't think we can help you any more. The thing's been done, hasn't it? I've got some arrangements to make." Mr Parker spoke bluntly, his keen blue eyes shining fiercely from his weather-beaten face.

Outside, the inspector frowned and leaned in silence over the fence opposite the cottage staring at the distant Cotswolds.

"Not much there!" he said.

"They have just lost their daughter, sir," commented P.C. Graham pointedly.

"All right, Constable, we 'foreigners' can be human you know. But hang it all, here's an attractive girl of 20 – was it? – and according to her father, she didn't seem to have had a friend or even a close acquaintance. What's the matter with Meadowvale, Graham?"

This burst of feeling from his sleepy-looking superior startled P.C. Graham.

"Well, it's partly her father, sir. He's a bit strict, you know. Regular churchgoer he is." P.C. Graham sniffed loudly. "I still think it was—"

"A 'foreigner?'," added Inspector Bancroft forcefully. He turned towards the constable and tugged at his moustache. "Well now, Graham. Since we have little other information at present, let's suppose that Dr Carlton's account is accurate. This quiet girl is murdered at 11.30 p.m. on a night as black as pitch, half a mile outside the village. Her only resistance: one short scream. What does that suggest to you?"

Debate with a superior, over evidence, was clearly

quite unfamiliar to P.C. Graham. "Well, he attacked her suddenly."

"What would the daughter of a father like Mr Parker be doing in a deserted road at that hour?"

P.C. Graham's face gave strong evidence of unaccustomed mental exertion.

"Perhaps she went for a walk," he spluttered. Then, under Inspector Bancroft's bushy gaze, he changed his mind. "No! Perhaps she went to meet somebody."

The inspector's pouchy face creased in approval.

"There may be a career in C.I.D. for you yet! And who do you think she might have gone to meet?"

With the whole world of 'foreigners' to choose from the constable's newfound power failed him.

"Well Graham, I suggest that she must have met someone she knew well. And with her limited experience of travel 'abroad' that probably means someone from the village.

"Someone who she could walk with and talk to without alarm or suspicion, someone who, at a certain place half a mile down that road, could attack and kill her with no more alarm being raised than a short cry."

P.C. Graham's eyes bulged in disbelief. Wicked logic of this sort was quite beyond him. Before he could speak Mrs Parker appeared at the inspector's elbow. She glanced furtively back at the house—her drawn face seemed to have grown more haggard in the few minutes since they had left.

"I found this in Fay's room," she said pushing a scrap of paper into the inspector's hand. "I didn't tell Bert about it."

She scuttled back into the cottage. After a brief glance, the inspector handed the paper to P.C. Graham.

'Same place. Tonight. 10.30. C.' The constable slowly read the note aloud. "C," he said, "could be Carlton."

"Or Clarendon," added the inspector, "don't forget the car the good doctor thought he recognised. Lead on Graham, let's pay our respects to the squire."

Inspector Bancroft halted the police car just beyond the main gate entrance to Hayes Farm, Clarendon's home. The pleasant walk along the long tree-lined drive on a delightful spring day appealed to him.

P.C. Graham clearly thought that sweeping up in the car would make a more impressive arrival. He was also doubtful of the inspector's crumpled and shabby raincoat.

Hayes Farm was not aptly named. The house itself, set in three acres of landscaped parkland, was an Elizabethan manor building. The road was quickly abandoned, and the inspector trudged on across the open lawns. P.C. Graham anxiously wondered if he dared suggest that they should approach the house from the front.

A broad, flagged terrace flanked the whole side of the house and the men made for this through a small ornamental garden. On the steps to the terrace, the inspector stopped and motioned P.C. Graham to stand still. Raised voices could be clearly heard coming from open French windows ahead.

"And I won't have you taking his part, do you understand!" said a man's voice trembling with anger.

"I shall choose my friends where I please. And I

63

don't want to be advised on what is right and wrong." The woman's reply was somewhat restrained and the more effective for it.

Inspector Bancroft glanced at P.C. Graham. "The Clarendons?"

Graham nodded. He was alarmed at the consequences should anyone come out onto the terrace.

"Shouldn't we go round to the door?" he asked. The inspector waved him to silence.

"I have a position to maintain here, and I have a right to expect full support from you," the man said.

"Position," the woman replied scornfully, "you haven't the least idea how to keep up a position. Anyone with an atom of sense could see right through you— you're a fake."

"You're in league with that blasted quack. He's put these ideas into your head. I'll see about him."

"Don't try that superior tone with me. You think I don't know about your damned women up and down the country. And you talk about the doctor and your position."

"Want anything?" A strongly built man of about 30 was standing by the shrubbery to the right.

P.C. Graham flushed bright pink and hung his mouth open to speak. "We – Barnes – we…"

"I'm Inspector Bancroft," the inspector intervened with a broad smile. "I've come to see Mr Clarendon. And – er – you are?"

"Looks like you're snooping to me," the young man snapped coldly.

"This is Barnes Carter, sir. He's Mr Clarendon's steward," P.C. Graham felt he had to redeem the police force from the inspector's bad manners.

"I'll tell him you're here!" Carter said.

"Before you go, Mr Carter," said the inspector intercepting him, "I should have to see you anyway. Perhaps we can save time, two birds with one stone."

"What do you want me for?"

"You've heard what happened last night, Mr Carter. I shall be seeing everybody sooner or later."

Carter barely restrained a comment.

"Where were you last night, Mr Carter, from about nine o'clock onwards?"

"At home; I was there from six o'clock – all evening – as soon as I finished work. I was in bed by 10."

"Your wife would have been with you?"

"I'm not married!"

"Hm! Where do you live, Mr Carter?"

"I have one of the bungalows on the estate!"

"It's just up the road from The Plough, sir," P.C. Graham explained.

"Is it now? You didn't happen to hear anything of what happened?"

"I told you, I was in bed and asleep by 10."

"Oh! Yes. That's right. And, of course, after a heavy day's work in the open air, you're a sound sleeper."

The inspector smiled at Carter and tugged at his moustache.

P.C. Graham doffed his helmet in the presence of the squire—something he hadn't thought necessary at the

65

Parkers. The Clarendons had positioned themselves to receive the police. Mrs Clarendon, an elegant woman of about 30, was seated on the edge of a vast chintzy settee. Her husband, in immaculate riding gear, stood by the stone fireplace. He was short and stocky; a good 10 years older than his wife.

"I believe the girl worked here," stated the inspector after a few aloof preliminaries had been dispensed with.

"Yes, she helped Mrs Gregory, our housekeeper," replied Mrs Clarendon, with a direct glance at her husband.

"What sort of girl did you find her to be, Mrs Clarendon?"

"She was a very quiet girl. I scarcely noticed her around the house most of the time. Though, of course, Inspector, you know what they say about still waters," Mrs Clarendon added as her last remark in a bitter tone.

Inspector Bancroft grunted awkwardly through his moustache. "Do you have any particular reason for saying that, Mrs Clarendon?"

"No! I just rarely take things at their face value." She directed such a frank gaze at the inspector, seated at the other end of the settee, that he shuffled his feet uneasily.

"Could I ask you, sir, where you were last night?"

"Are we under some kind of suspicion?" demanded Mr Clarendon.

Inspector Bancroft felt that his irate tone was more the result of his wife's manner than the question.

"Just routine, sir. We like to establish a clear picture of events right from the start."

"We were at home all evening."

The inspector glanced apologetically at Mrs Clarendon.

"That's right."

P.C. Graham coughed nervously and then apologised for interrupting.

"Well, I think that's all for now," said the inspector, "may we walk back to the gate across your lawn? As you can see, I need the exercise. So does P.C. Graham here, for that matter." He patted his bulging and slightly stained waistcoat.

For a while, P.C. Graham plodded silently beside the inspector. At last, he could restrain himself no longer.

"Beg your pardon, sir, but I was wondering why you didn't ask Mr Clarendon about the car?"

"You're not suggesting that the 'squire' would mislead us, are you Graham?"

"Er – No – No, sir!"

P.C. Graham's expression showed that he was rather confused by the message from County Police Headquarters.

Two days later the inspector was sitting in the bar parlour of The Plough, finishing off his extensive plateful of eggs and bacon. The day before, Charlie Draycott had offered the inspector any services of this sort that he might need. Charlie Draycott was about 40, inclining to fat and bristling with a huge handlebar moustache. He had scarcely stopped talking since Inspector Bancroft had knocked at the rear door half an hour earlier.

"Would you like any more, Inspector?" he asked from across the table, "the wife could have them out in no time at all."

"No! No! Thank you. I shall be sorry to leave Meadowvale—if only because I shall miss your wife's cooking."

"Oh! Will you be going soon, then? I always said it was a 'foreigner' who did it. I don't suppose there's much sense wasting much more time around here?"

Inspector Bancroft smiled and wiped the straggling fringe of his moustache thoroughly. Charlie had been attempting to entice information out of him throughout the breakfast.

"I don't think we've finished here yet, Mr Draycott," the inspector said. He crossed to the parlour window and stared down the road.

"I suppose this is the nearest building to where it happened?" he said.

"Well, apart from Barnes Carter's cottage. That's off the road and up the track to the estate."

"Oh! Yes. You didn't see any strangers in here on Monday night?"

"No, we don't get many strangers coming through Meadowvale. It's not on the main road, you see. And Monday is always a quiet night."

"I don't suppose you heard anything after you locked up?"

"No. First thing I knew about it was when John – er P.C. Graham – knocked me up. Near enough midnight that would be."

Punctually at nine o'clock, P.C. Graham arrived. He was not surprised that his eccentric superior should

68

arrange to meet him at a pub at that hour of the morning.

"We should be just in time to interrupt Dr Carlton's surgery again," the inspector confided to P.C. Graham after Charlie Draycott had unwillingly withdrawn from the parlour.

As they paraded on show up the village street, Inspector Bancroft revealed the latest items of information.

P.C. Graham's large face assumed a smug expression. "I thought so," he stated.

Dr Carlton's greeting was as brusque as on the first occasion.

"Did you know that Parker was pregnant?" the inspector asked at length. Dr Carlton was unmoved by the question and nodded curtly.

"Why didn't you tell me?"

"You were sure to find out," the doctor said briskly, "And I don't regard it as my duty to reveal confidential information about my patients."

"Even when they end up murdered less than a mile from your front door?!" snapped the inspector with a burst of emotion which took P.C. Graham, at least, by surprise.

"Especially then," replied Dr Carlton, unimpressed, "the poor girl's death will set enough tongues wagging in this place without my adding fuel to the fire. Have you ever thought about her parents' feelings?"

"I have, sir," answered the inspector drily, "I suppose the girl was in something of a state about her condition."

"She was desperate."

"Did she mention who was responsible?"

"No! And I don't care to speculate!"

"I suppose, being a conscientious doctor, you gave her good advice?"

"I told her to tell her parents and make damned sure the man – whoever he was – didn't escape his responsibilities."

"Did she tell her parents?"

"I doubt it. Bert Parker isn't exactly ideally cast for the role of understanding father."

"So you tried to offer her the understanding you didn't think she'd get at home?"

Dr Carlton slammed his fist down on the desk. "Yes! And you can damned well make anything of it you like!" Inspector Bancroft slumped even further into the cane chair.

"I believe you had dinner together once or twice in Bracehampton?"

"Yes, what of it?"

"You were a friend in need, Doctor?"

Dr Carlton's eyes blazed with anger.

P.C. Graham by the door felt that he might be called on to rescue his superior at any moment. The telephone intervened.

"Hello!" Dr Carlton shouted into it. "I'll be right there," he said after listening intently then put the phone down. Turning to the inspector he said, "That was Barnes Carter. One of Clarendon's men, Williams, has had an accident with a tractor up near Boulder Pasture. He thinks his head might be injured. May I go?"

Inspector Bancroft nodded amicably. "Of course, you must do your duty."

With a snort of utter distaste, Dr Carlton seized his

bag and left. For a moment, Inspector Bancroft remained in place.

"Do you know Boulder Pasture?" he asked.

"Yes. It's about a mile past The Plough—up Rectory Lane," P.C. Graham replied.

"Right! We'll go there!"

P.C. Graham gave directions to the police driver. As the car moved off, he saw a van parked outside the village general store.

"There's Barnes Carter's van!" he cried.

Barnes Carter himself staggered through the shop door with a large bag of fertiliser in his arms. He glared sourly at the police car as it passed by. P.C. Graham turned in bewilderment to the inspector behind him.

"All right, Graham, calm down. I didn't think Carter made the call just now."

P.C. Graham's mouth opened and closed in silence.

"Don't forget that the murderer saw Dr Carlton find the girl's body. He may feel himself in danger and I think he's about to try to get out of it."

There was no traffic on the narrow, turning country road. The car hurtled past the place where the girl's body was found and slowed noisily into Rectory Lane at the crossroads. After the church disappeared from view behind, P.C. Graham called to the driver to stop. Dr Carlton's small red car was parked on the roadside verge near a gate.

"Look," P.C. Graham called, pointing to the large field beyond the hedge.

Dr Carlton's body was motionless in the grass. Standing over him was Bert Parker raising a large rock in his hand.

"Stop!" shouted Inspector Bancroft.

Parker dropped the rock and stood calmly waiting for the police to take him.

"Two sins," he said, "both paid for in full."

Before leaving Meadowvale, Inspector Bancroft invited P.C. Graham for a farewell drink at The Plough. There was some initial confusion as P.C. Graham became accustomed to the idea of drinking socially with an inspector.

"I don't think we need make any further enquiries," Inspector Bancroft said after draining a pint of bitter, "but I think Mrs Clarendon's assessment of her husband's behaviour is not very far off the mark."

"But Bert Parker," said P.C. Graham shaking his head, "how could he do it? His own daughter."

"It seems he was obsessed by the idea of sin and punishment. My guess is that Fay Parker had a meeting with Clarendon somewhere in the village at 10.30 p.m. After that meeting, or possibly before, maybe after her heart-to-heart talks with Dr Carlton, she told her father. You can imagine the effect it must have had on a man of his views. Clarendon may have decided to come back again. Perhaps he had resolved to act nobly—that we shall never know. What he saw in those car headlights scared him off."

The inspector winked at a startled P.C. Graham.

"At any rate, we know it wasn't a 'foreigner'," he said.